My Home Country

SOUTH AFRICA

IS MY HOME

To Tumi and her generation of all races as they grow up in the new South Africa.

For a free color catalog describing Gareth Stevens' list of high quality books, call 1-800-341-3569 (USA) or 1-800-461-9120 (Canada).

For their help in the preparation of *South Africa Is My Home,* the editors gratefully thank the Milwaukee Public Library; the International Institute of Wisconsin, Milwaukee; and Peter Kwele. The author and photographer thank Peter Celliers of Ellis Associates in New York; Jimmy Ntintile of Face to Face Tours in Johannesburg; Bettie Wessels of SATOUR in Johannesburg; and South African Airways, each of whom assisted us in ways far beyond our travel arrangements.

Flag illustration on page 42, © Flag Research Center.

Library of Congress Cataloging-in-Publication Data

Daniel, Jamie.
        South Africa is my home / adapted from Barbara Radcliffe Rogers' Children of the world--South Africa by Jamie Daniel ; photographs by Stillman Rogers.
                p.   cm. -- (My home country)
        Includes bibliographical references and index.
        Summary: Presents the life of a twelve-year-old girl who lives in Soweto, a suburb of Johannesburg, under a system of apartheid. Includes a reference section with information about South Africa.
        ISBN 0-8368-0851-7
        1. South Africa--Social life and customs--Juvenile literature. 2. Children--South Africa--Juvenile literature. 3. Children, Black--South Africa--Juvenile literature. 4. Soweto (South Africa) --Social life and customs--Juvenile literature. 5. Children--South Africa--Soweto--Juvenile literature. 6. Children, Black--South Africa--Soweto--Juvenile literature. [1. South Africa--Social life and customs. 2. Motube, Tumi. 3. Blacks--South Africa.]
        I. Rogers, Stillman, 1939- ill. II. Rogers, Barbara Radcliffe. South Africa. III. Title. IV. Series.
        DT1752.D36   1992
        968--dc20   92-17722

Edited, designed, and produced by

Gareth Stevens Publishing
1555 North RiverCenter Drive, Suite 201
Milwaukee, WI 53212, USA

Text, photographs, and format © 1992 by Gareth Stevens, Inc. First published in the United States and Canada in 1992 by Gareth Stevens, Inc. This U.S. edition is abridged from *Children of the World: South Africa,* © 1990 by Gareth Stevens, Inc., with text by Barbara Radcliffe Rogers and photographs by Stillman Rogers.

Series editor: Beth Karpfinger
Cover design: Kristi Ludwig
Designer: Sabine Huschke
Map design: Sheri Gibbs

Printed in the United States of America

1 2 3 4 5 6 7 8 9 9 97 96 95 94 93 92

SOUTH AFRICA

IS MY HOME

Adapted from Barbara Radcliffe Rogers'
Children of the World: South Africa

by Jamie Daniel
Photographs by Stillman Rogers

Gareth Stevens Publishing
MILWAUKEE

Tumi Motube is a 12-year-old girl from Soweto, an area outside of Johannesburg, where she and her mother live in one small room. Tumi, a black girl, lives under the system of apartheid, a separation of the races according to skin color. She helps her mother with household chores, does the marketing, and cooks special dishes.

To enhance this book's value in libraries and classrooms, clear and simple reference sections include up-to-date information about South African geography, demographics, languages, currency, education, culture, industry, and natural resources. *South Africa Is My Home* also features a large and colorful map, a bibliography, glossary, simple index, and activity projects designed especially for young readers.

The living conditions and experiences of children in South Africa vary according to economic, environmental, and ethnic circumstances. The reference sections help bring to life for young readers the diversity and richness of the culture and heritage of South Africa. Of particular interest are discussions of South Africa's tribal history, natural resources, government, and its long and exciting history.

My Home Country includes the following titles:

Canada	*Nicaragua*
Costa Rica	*Peru*
Cuba	*Poland*
El Salvador	*South Africa*
Guatemala	*Vietnam*
Ireland	*Zambia*

CONTENTS

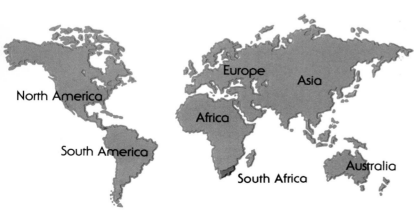

North America

South America

Europe

Asia

Africa

South Africa

Australia

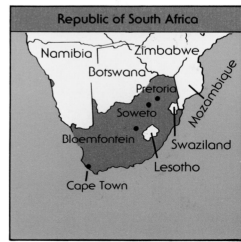

Republic of South Africa

Namibia

Zimbabwe

Botswana

Mozambique

Pretoria

Soweto

Swaziland

Bloemfontein

Lesotho

Cape Town

LIFE IN SOUTH AFRICA:

Tumi, a Girl from Soweto

Tumi Motube is twelve years old. She lives with her mother in Soweto, just outside the city of Johannesburg.

"Tumi" is a nickname for the name Boitumelo (boy-TOO-meh-low), Tumi's middle name. This name means "happiness" in the Tswana language.

Tumi and her mother share a happy moment.

Life in Soweto

Soweto (so-WEH-toe) is a nickname, too. It is made up of the first letters of SOuth WEstern TOwnships. Townships are poor areas where black South Africans live. Blacks do not have the same freedoms that whites have. The system that created different rules for blacks and whites is called "apartheid" (a-PART-hide). The word means "separateness" in the Afrikaans language.

Right: Fences in Soweto are made of whatever people can find.
Inset: Slogans like this protest apartheid.
Below: Many people in Soweto share toilets and water faucets.

The home Tumi shares with her mother has only one room. But it is in one of the nicer neighborhoods in Soweto. Nelson Mandela, a famous black leader, once lived nearby. But not all Soweto neighborhoods are as nice as this one.

In poorer parts of the township, many little houses are crowded together on lots meant for just one home. Sometimes many people must share one toilet and one water supply.

People in the township spend much of their time outdoors. ▸
Below: This big home in Soweto once belonged to Nelson Mandela.

Parts of Soweto are crowded with home-less people who came to the city looking for jobs. These people set up shacks wher-ever they find room. They are called squatters.

The government forces squatters out of their shacks. But because there is nowhere for them to go, the squatters simply "squat" else-where. When Tumi passes their camps, she feels lucky to have a home.

A typical squatter camp. Inset: Children from the squatter camp on their way to nursery school.

Tumi's mother, Elizabeth, works at a hairdresser's shop in town. She must take a bus from Soweto to get to her job. The trip takes an hour each way.

Tumi and her mother once lived with Elizabeth's parents in a town called Kimberley. When Elizabeth had to move to Soweto to find work in Johannesburg, Tumi stayed behind with her grandparents.

But Tumi and her mother missed each other so much that they decided Tumi would move to Soweto, too. Now, whenever they have vacations, they take the train to Kimberley to visit Tumi's grandparents.

Tumi often has dinner ready by the time her mother gets home from work. ▶

14

Like many townships, Soweto has both nice neighborhoods and very poor neighborhoods.

At Home with Tumi

Tumi and her mother share one bed that is also used as a couch. Here, Tumi does her homework in the evening.

Tumi and Elizabeth cook their meals on a hot plate and wash the dishes in the bathroom sink. While their home is small, Tumi and her mother also spend time in the yard.

Tumi tells her mother about her day.

Once Tumi is ready for bed, she reads before going to sleep.

A Busy Morning

Tumi and her mother get up at 6:00 a.m. to have breakfast together. After her mother leaves for work, Tumi washes the dishes. Then she packs her books and lunch and leaves for school. She hurries so she'll have time to play with her friends on the playground before school starts. They play jump rope or dodgeball.

Top inset: Tumi irons her blouse for school.
Bottom inset: Tumi carries her books and lunch in a canvas shoulder bag.
Tumi tries to duck the ball during a game of dodgeball. ▶

Boepakitso School

Tumi goes to Boepakitso School. *Boepakitso* means "digging for knowledge." Some of Tumi's classmates are older than she is, and some are younger. This is because older black children must sometimes stay home to babysit so their parents can work. This means they get a later start on school.

Inset: Children have planted a garden around the school sign. Below: The Boepakitso School is in a modern building.

Mr. Leteate teaches the class about the parts of a leaf.

Tumi's teachers are Mr. Leteate and Mr. Mbuyisa. Tumi and her friends like to take part in class discussions. They know that a good education will help them get ahead when they are older.

Both black and white children in South Africa learn English and Afrikaans. At Tumi's school, children also learn Tswana, the language spoken by the black people in the Transvaal, the area around Johannesburg. Afrikaans is the language spoken by the white Dutch settlers of South Africa.

The children study all morning, and then they have a lunch break. Some children go home for lunch, others bring a bag lunch, and some buy a hot lunch near school.

These are the books Tumi brings home from school each night.

After lunch, Tumi and her friends dance or play in the schoolyard. When the bell rings, they return to class until 2:00 p.m., when school ends.

Tumi and her friends dance during recess.

Classes end at 2:00 p.m., but school stays open until 5:00 p.m. so children can do their homework. The teachers also stay late to help them with their assignments. Many children do homework at school because they don't have a quiet space at home.

Here is a crossword puzzle that Tumi did for social studies class.

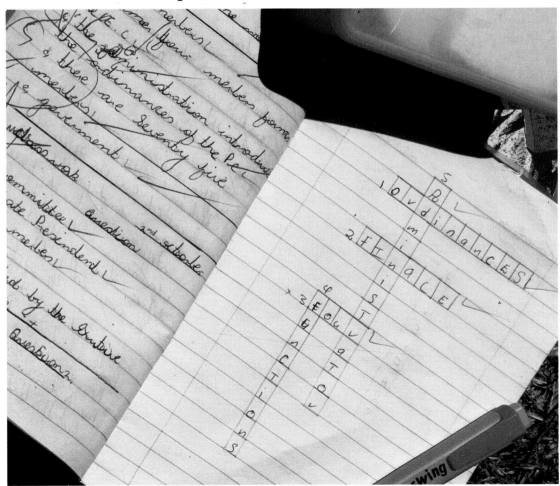

Tumi and Mr. Leteate talk about the news articles.

Sometimes Tumi stays after school to talk with her teachers or to help put news stories on the school bulletin board.

Shopping After School

When Tumi has extra "carry money," she may stop on the way home from school for french fries or hot fried bread.

Tumi likes to eat french fries as an after-school snack.

Tumi's mother has taught her how to shop at the supermarket.

Because of the long bus ride, Tumi's mother doesn't get home from work until 7:00 p.m. So it is Tumi's job to buy groceries and make dinner. She has learned from her mother how to choose fresh vegetables and meat.

The supermarket is located in a shopping mall. Tumi likes to window shop at the clothing stores after buying her groceries.

Like malls in North America, this one has many fast-food shops. Before returning home, Tumi sometimes buys an ice cream.

After shopping, Tumi has money left for a treat — ice cream!

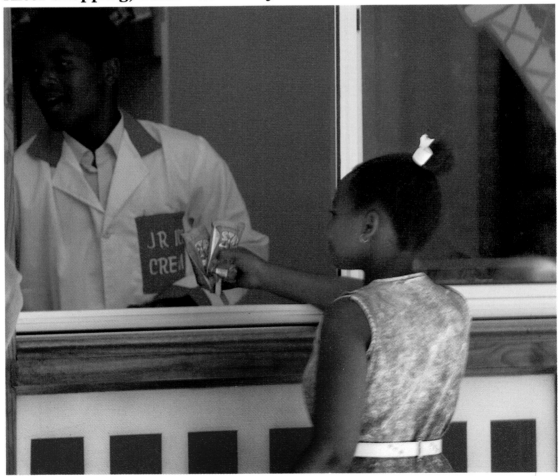

Tumi likes to window shop for clothes at the mall.

The Outdoor Market

Soweto also has vendors who gather outside to sell fresh fruits and vegetables. Vendors also sell clothing, candy, and meat. The meat cooks on open grills called *brais*.

There are also vendors who sell roots and unusual plants. These are *dinkatas*, people who have learned to cure illnesses with herbs and plants. They learn this skill from parents and grandparents who were also dinkatas.

**Farmers sell their crops in the outdoor markets.
Inset: A *dinkata* sells herbs and plants.**

Each stand at the market is like a little store. Some stands sell spices. Others sell fresh fish, chickens, or flowers.

The vendors come from many different areas of South Africa. Tumi may see women wearing Malaysian dress or Shangan women wrapped in blankets. The market is noisy with the many languages of South Africa.

Above: An Indian market. Below: Hot peppers are used in traditional African foods. This vendor sells row after row of colorful flowers. ▶

The Food Tumi Eats

Tumi and her mother eat foods that come from their Tswana culture and the many other cultures that live together in South Africa. For example, immigrants from India introduced the curried foods that are now eaten all over South Africa.

Many South African dishes combine meats and vegetables. Tumi and her mother also eat fried sweet potatoes and a spicy dish called "yellow rice." Tumi's favorite food is steak cooked on a brai.

Meat cooking over a brai.

Above: *Babootie,* a dish made of ground meat with bay leaves.
Below: Spicy side dishes to go with an Indian meal.

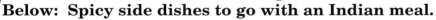

The Many Peoples of South Africa

Many black South African children have grown up in cities. They live far from the villages of their ancestors. Their history lives on through stories and songs.

One group that is keeping its history alive is the Zulus. They welcome visitors to their dances and celebrations.

Many South African tribes make beautiful beadwork. ▶
Below: This Zulu dance tells about events in Zulu history.

In South Africa, people belong to many racial groups and speak different languages. One hears Zulu and other black languages, as well as Afrikaans, English, and the languages of India and Malaysia.

It is exciting living in a country with so many cultures, especially now that the apartheid laws are changing and nonwhites have more freedom. Tumi is proud that her country is changing for the better.

This background is beautiful cloth made by a country weaver. Below: The Ndebele people give these dolls to new brides.

MORE FACTS ABOUT: South Africa

Official Name: Republic of South Africa

Capitals: Pretoria, Cape Town,
            and Bloemfontein

History

Scientists believe that prehistoric human ancestors lived in South Africa two million years ago. By the year AD 1200, many tribes from the north began to move southward. These migrants became the Zulu, Tsonga, Sotho, Swazi, Tswana, Venda, and Xhosa peoples. By the time the first Europeans arrived in 1488, eastern South Africa was home to these tribes.

People from Holland came to South Africa in 1652. They forced black tribes from their own land. Britain took over the Dutch Cape Colony in 1794. The Dutch settlers, called "Afrikaners," left to settle new lands in the north. By the 1850s, South Africa had split into four colonies. Tensions between the Afrikaners and British grew, and in 1899, war broke out. The Afrikaners surrendered in 1902, and South Africa became a British colony. The British agreed to some demands made by the Afrikaners. One was that blacks not be allowed to vote. The white minority set up a group of laws called apartheid.

Apartheid kept apart blacks, whites, and people with mixed backgrounds. Many blacks, other people of color, and whites protested, and many people were imprisoned and killed. Nelson Mandela, the leader of the African National Congress (ANC), was sentenced to life in prison. Several countries refused to recognize South Africa until the laws were changed. In 1990, Mandela was freed, and today, little by little, the apartheid system is changing.

Land and Climate

The sea surrounds South Africa on three sides. Much of the country is flat and desertlike, but there are also rolling grasslands. Beautiful mountain ranges are found where the two types of land meet. Because South Africa is south of the equator, it is warmest in December and coldest in June and July.

People and Languages

Of the 37 million people in South Africa, 74% are black, 14% are white, 9% are "coloured," or of mixed background, and 3% are Indian. Whites descend from Dutch or British settlers. Blacks have their own tribal languages. Many also understand the language of the Zulu, South Africa's biggest tribe. Most blacks also speak English, and often different groups of blacks talk to each other only in English or Afrikaans.

Education

The government of South Africa has not required education for blacks, but as more black teachers are trained, more black children are able to go to school. Today, 80% of black children attend school.

Religion

More than 75% of South Africans, both black and white, are Christian. There is also a small Jewish community. Most Asian South Africans are Hindus, but some are Muslim or Christian. Traditional tribal religions are also practiced.

Sports and Recreation

Soccer is the most popular sport in South Africa. There are over one hundred soccer fields in Soweto alone. Girls rarely take part in competitive sports.

South Africans in North America

Few South Africans lived in North America before 1976. But as racial tensions increased, more whites moved away. Now about 850 South Africans of all races move to the U.S. and Canada each year.

South African currency.

Glossary of Useful South African Terms

apartheid: South African laws that deny blacks most rights enjoyed by whites.

brai: an outdoor grill used for cooking meat.

dinkata: someone trained to use plants for medicine.

More Books About South Africa

Journey to Jo'burg: A South African Story. Naidoo (Harper Junior Books)
We Live in South Africa. Kristensen (FranklinWatts)

Things to Do

1. Draw a map of South Africa showing where it is in the world. What are the names of the countries that border it?

2. Wouldn't you like to find out more about life in South Africa from someone living there? Get the address of a pen pal by writing to this organization: Worldwide Pen Friends, P.O. Box 39097, Downey, CA 90241.

Be sure to tell them which country you want your pen pal to be from, and always include your name, address, and age.

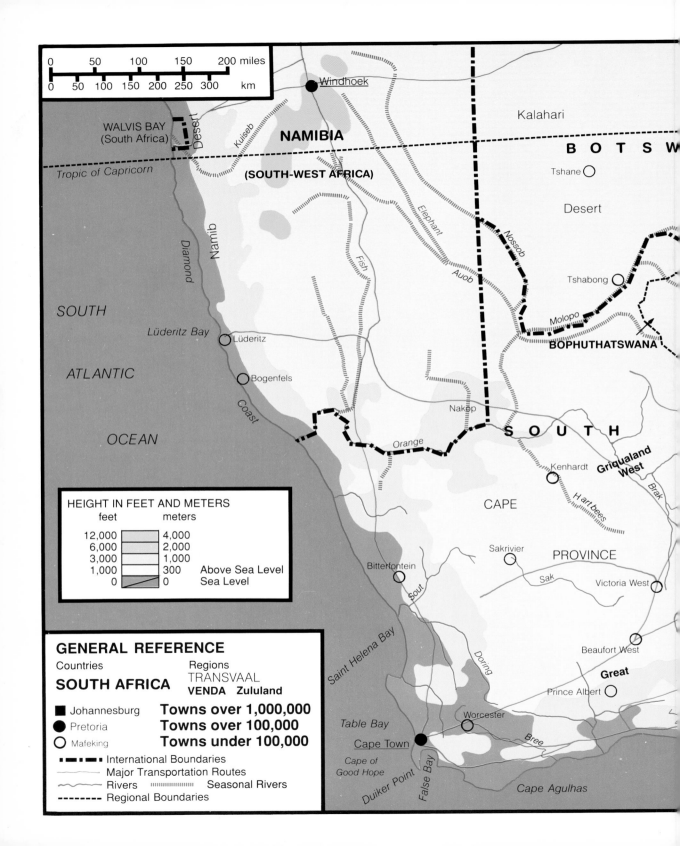

Windhoek

Kalahari

NAMIBIA

B O T S W

(SOUTH-WEST AFRICA)

Desert

Tshane ○

WALVIS BAY
(South Africa)

Desert

Tropic of Capricorn

Kuiseb

Namib

Elephant

Nossob

Fish

Auob

Tshabong ○

SOUTH

Diamond

Molopo

ATLANTIC

Lüderitz Bay ○ Lüderitz

BOPHUTHATSWANA

Bogenfels ○

Nakop

S O U T H

OCEAN

Coast

Orange

Kenhardt ○

Griqualand West

Brak

CAPE

Hartbees

Sakrivier ○

PROVINCE

Victoria West ○

HEIGHT IN FEET AND METERS

feet   meters

12,000   4,000
6,000   2,000
3,000   1,000
1,000   300   Above Sea Level
0   0   Sea Level

Sak

Bitterfontein ○

Sout

Beaufort West ○

Saint Helena Bay

Doring

Great

Prince Albert ○

GENERAL REFERENCE

Countries   Regions
SOUTH AFRICA   TRANSVAAL
                       VENDA Zululand

Table Bay

Worcester ○

Cape Town ●

■ Johannesburg   **Towns over 1,000,000**
● Pretoria   **Towns over 100,000**
○ Mafeking   **Towns under 100,000**

Cape of
Good Hope

Bree

────── International Boundaries
────── Major Transportation Routes
～～～ Rivers   ▨▨▨▨ Seasonal Rivers
─ ─ ─ Regional Boundaries

Duiker Point

False Bay

Cape Agulhas

0   50   100   150   200 miles
0   50 100 150 200 250 300 km

SOUTH AFRICA — Political and Physical

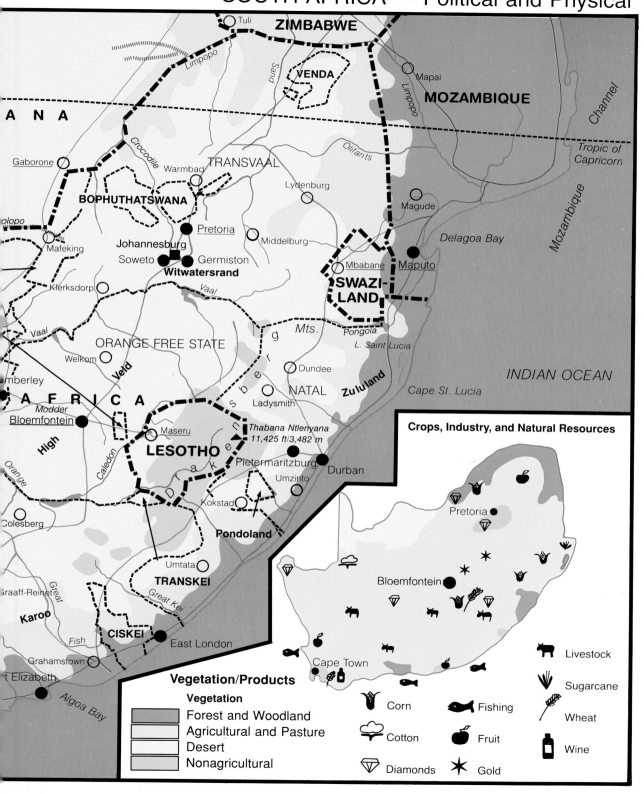

ZIMBABWE

Tuli

VENDA

MOZAMBIQUE

Mapai

Limpopo

Sand

Limpopo

Tropic of Capricorn

Channel

Gaborone

Crocodile

TRANSVAAL

Warmbad

Olifants

Lydenburg

Magude

Delagoa Bay

Mozambique

BOPHUTHATSWANA

olopo

Mafeking

Pretoria

Johannesburg

Middelburg

Mbabane

Maputo

Soweto

Germiston

SWAZI-LAND

Witwatersrand

Klerksdorp

Vaal

Pongola

L. Saint Lucia

Vaal

ORANGE FREE STATE

Mts.

INDIAN OCEAN

Welkom

Veld

berg

Dundee

Cape St. Lucia

mberley

AFRICA

High

Modder

Bloemfontein

Maseru

LESOTHO

Ladysmith

NATAL

Zululand

Thabana Ntlenyana
11,425 ft/3,482 m

Pietermaritzburg

Durban

Umzinto

Orange

Caledon

Drakensberg

Kokstad

Colesberg

Pondoland

Great

Graaff-Reinet

Umtata

TRANSKEI

Great Kei

Karoo

CISKEI

East London

Fish

Grahamstown

t Elizabeth

Algoa Bay

Crops, Industry, and Natural Resources

Pretoria

Bloemfontein

Cape Town

Vegetation/Products

Vegetation

Forest and Woodland
Agricultural and Pasture
Desert
Nonagricultural

Corn

Fishing

Cotton

Fruit

Diamonds

Gold

Livestock

Sugarcane

Wheat

Wine

Index